AF351222

A Mountain of Trouble

Al Vernon had come to Panama to get away from the crime and sordidity where he was a cop in Atlanta, Georgia.

He bought a ranch on Chorcha Mountain and settled down for a peaceful life. He was only 46 years old, and had raised his son and daughter. His wife had died in an accident he wouldn't talk about. It was too painful. He had always felt guilty that he wasn't there. That was part of why he left the police.

It seemed that peaceful wasn't in the cards for Al Vernon

A Mountain of Trouble
© 2018 by C. D. Moulton

all rights reserved: no part of this publication may be reproduced or transmitted in any form or by any means, electronic or mechanical, including photocopy, recording, or any information retrieval system, without permission in writing from the copyright holder/publisher, except in the case of brief quotations embodied in critical articles or reviews.

This is a work of fiction. Any resemblances to actual persons or events are purely coincidental unless otherwise stated.

Contents

About the author

CD Moulton has traveled extensively over much of the world both in the music business, where he was a rock guitarist, songwriter and arranger and in an import/export business. He has been everything from a bar owner to auto salvage (junkyard) manager, longshoreman to high steel worker, orchid grower to landscaper, tropical fish farmer to commercial fisherman. He started writing books in 1983 and has published more than 350 books as of January 1, 2023. His most popular books to date are about research with orchids, though much of his science fiction and fantasy work has proven popular. He wrote the CD Grimes, PI series, and the Det. Nick Storie series, Clint Faraday series, and many other works.

He now resides in Gualaca, Chiriqui, Panamá, where he writes books, plays music with friends, does research with orchids and medicinal plants. He has lately become involved in fighting for the rights of the indigenous people, who are among his closest friends, and in fighting the extreme corruption in the courts and police in Panamá.

He offers the free e-book, *Fading Paradise*, that explains what he has been through because of the corruption.

CD is the discoverer of the Chadam Protocol for curing cancer.

Facebook page Ambrosia peruviana for cancer.

<u>Arrival</u>

Alton (Al) Marcus Vernon, 46 years as of last month, ex cop, father, widowed, slung the backpack off his shoulders at the top of the long rough road to the top of Chorcha Mountain, Chiriqui, Panama, and looked back at the view. He could see, from his position, the Pacific Ocean, 34 miles away, the city of David, and Volcan Baru.

Here, at last.

It was quiet and peaceful. There was a light breeze. It had rained there last night. It was cool and clean.

He walked the trail across the large cow pasture and into the forest, about a kilometer, and then along the rough scraped off road to the west side of the mesa that was the top of Chorcha Mountain. He looked over the town of Los Angeles and the comarca land below.

Beautiful.

A bit farther on he came to his property. Though he hadn't wanted it, there was a fence. It was required to mark his property. 12 hectares of paradise!

The small cabin-type house fit the place. Just yesterday afternoon he had brought in the last of the furnishings and personal items. He had gone back with the delivery truck (that had carried the items only to the top. Horses carried everything from there to his cabin.) He spent the night in David, then rode a bus to the entrance to the road to the top.

Four hours of hiking, always upward, brought him to the top. He had only met seven of the Indios who lived on the mountain in that four hours. He had stopped to chat with all of them.

He was told the Indios would not accept a gringo living among them, and was afraid he would have trouble there – at first.

He met a few when he went to make the plano for the property. He had talked with them, and they became friends. These were a very open amicable people. He didn't understand why the gringos he'd met kept warning him about them.

He asked Bino (Balbino. They used the last part of the given name as a nickname, not the first) why the gringos said what they said. He got an answer that he soon learned was the kind of answer he would get from the people.

"You talk with us. They talk to us."

Straight up and to the point. He could guess the

condescension and arrogance they saw from most of the ones he talked to. He realized right then that they even talked "to" him, and not "with" him.

It reminded him of the same type of thing he read in a Clint Faraday mystery. Those stories were based, in many cases, on real events. A woman was ranting about the ignorant Indios in a condescending manner, based totally on her opinion and misinformation, about all the things they do, and all the things she "knew" about them. An eight year old Indio boy said, "Ignorance isn't about what you know. It's about what you don't know."

Al grinned at the description of the look on her face.

Bino helped build the small cabin. They became friends. Bino's wife, Amaia, cooked meals for him, and his two sons and daughter helped with the work. Al was amazed at how a six year old boy could pick up and carry a weight he struggled with.

"It's because you don't carry it right. You carry it with your arms and legs, we carry it with our back."

He didn't know what that meant. He always carried heavy weights with his back.

"No, you put it on your shoulders, but you lean forward under the weight and make your legs carry it."

He let the boy show him what he meant. It was surprising how much easier it was if you were straight up.

"See? You lean forward and you're using you back to try to balance it, which your legs have to do the whole time you're carrying it, so they have to do both. Your arms have to keep the shifting weight with each step, so they get tired. If the weight is balanced on your shoulders all you have to do with your legs is walk, and your arms just hold it there."

Hard to describe what they meant. Easy to demonstrate.

Al grinned again and took his backpack inside to toss it on the bed. He went into the kitchen and lit the stove to brew some coffee – from plants that were growing just outside the back door. He went to the refrigerator, to see that there were several items he didn't put there, and a couple were missing.

That is the Indio way. They shared, you shared. It was part of their culture.

The refrigerator was his only thing most didn't have here. He put in a solar panel on the roof for it, and a couple of light bulbs. He didn't want or have a TV. He had a cheap cell phone, simply as a matter of practicality.

He did *not* have locks on his doors. People could come and go as they pleased.

"Oye, Tio Al!" came from the door. He looked to see a boy of about eight years of age coming in with a bolsa. He raised an eyebrow. [Hi, Uncle Al!]

"Para la refri," Jorge [the boy] explained, and put the bolsa in the freezer part. "Pollo, y poco iguana."

[For keeping in the refrigerator. Chicken, with some iguana.]

"Hay espacio?" [Is there room?]

He shrugged, and looked inside, then put the bag in. "Si. Bastante!"

[Yes. Plenty!]

He waved and went back out. Al shook his head and smiled. This was as much proof they considered him "family" as he could ask for.

He went to the bedroom, undressed, and took a long cool [Well, cold, actually] shower. He laid on the bed to relax and rest a bit before unpacking the things still in cartons. Jorge came in and climbed on the bed with him. "Tiene suenos?" [Are you sleepy?]

"Solo poco consado." [Just a little tired.]

Jorge laid against him. He thought of what any gringo would think, him in his skivvies, laying in bed with an eight year old boy, and giggled.

"Que?" [What?]

"Nada. Que otra gingos crea." [Nothing. What other gringos would think.]

"De que?" [About what?]

"Vida." [Life.]

Jorge grinned and leaned tighter against him. He felt a flush of affection for the boy. The Indios were a touching people. It was affection, both ways.

"Mas tardes es un sorprisa. Mama y Yvet prepara. Yvet legusta te mucho." [Later is a surprise. Mama and Yvet are making it. Yvet really likes you.]

"Yvet? La nina bonita? Ella es, que? diez y siete?" [Yvet? The pretty girl? She is what? Seventeen?]

"Diez y ocho. Es legal aqui, ahora!" [Eighteen. She is legal age (age of consent) here, now!]

"Pero yo esta cuarente seis!" [But I'm forty six!]

"Y?" [And?]

He tousled Jorge's thick black hair. "Y legal en la comarca?" [And legal in the comarca?]

"Doce." [Twelve.]

He hugged Jorge. They dozed for a few minutes, then got up to do the unpacking.

[I will translate from this point. The conversations were, in most parts, in Spanish or Guayme.]

"I think that about does it for where I want everything. Tomorrow I can start planting the things I want close to the house."

Jorge looked around, and nodded. "It's practical and comfortable. Like a home, not just a house.

"Tio Al, I have to work tomorrow, but Beto and Santo can help, if you want."

That was serious. Eight years old, and he had his job and responsibilities.

"I want to know what I can do in the community. I want to be part of it, not just some gringo who lives here."

"We know. Gilda says you helped with the water pump thing, and there will be electricity soon for the whole mountain, so you will be good for that. I don't know if the electricity is good."

"It's good for some things. No so much for others."

"Good for some people, and bad for others. Yes.

I think Mama will say it has to be only for the light at night. No television in her house, and you have the refrigerator we all use."

"We can make a little reservoir and can pump water to all the houses, and make bathrooms inside, like here. There's a natural sewage plant down off the ridge that won't contaminate anything. It's a natural settling pond that will feed into the cleft, then fall for more than a kilometer. It will be purified by the time it gets to the quebrada, and even drinkable before it gets to the river. It's straight up and down along there, and nobody lives in the quebrada. It's too steep and rocky. I have a lot of PVC we can use.

"I want everything to stay natural here."

"Yes. But you have to be practical. It's coming." (From an eight year old kid!)

"I'm used to it. I sort of wish I hadn't put any lights in this house. The practical part is the refrigerator."

"A light in the house is good. A lot of them isn't, like in Rincon, and worse in Chiriqui. Even Los Angeles, there are too many. One, outside, with a table – like you have in back, where we can sit and talk and joke and lie at night is good. A lot of them is bad. One, we come together. Many, we move apart. That is not good."

"I do not lie! The ten women who won't leave me alone is true!"

"And they're invisible!" Jorge gave him the finger. They both laughed.

"Well, let's shower and go to my house. Act surprised."

The party was a lot of fun. They had a bottle of rum, and everybody got a little drunk. The Indios have no natural resistance to alcohol. One drink, and they can't stop until they're plastered – so they had one bottle for everyone to have a little. He had a slight buzz, but wasn't really drunk. He had learned about the guava leaf extract from a character in Gualaca, so wouldn't have a hangover.

In the morning he went into the forest to collect some of the colorful plants that would cost a fortune in the states, but were almost weeds here. He had a flair for landscape, so it was going to be nice when it grew in. He used a lot of fruits and medicinal plants. Mangos and avocados, jobitos, an orange tree, a lemon tree, papayas, moringa, Ambrosia, pineapples, bananas, even a clump of mora (raspberries) that grew wild on the mountains. There was already a large guava tree and nance.

By about four o'clock he had it much the way he wanted it. He used some PVC to make a drip irrigation system until it all grew in. That would only be a couple of weeks, here. He thought of the saying, "If you want a certain plant or tree in Panama, stick a piece of limb in the ground and stand back." It was almost true. His fence posts were already sprouting. He would have to keep them trimmed. He would make a vegetable garden along the fence on the inland side. He wanted to grow okra and zucchini, which few grew here. There was a large melon [a type of sweet pumpkin] already there. It had two melons that would weigh fifty pounds apiece!

He cleaned up and went to Hanibal's house to chat awhile with several people, then went home. He slept very well. He only woke up once when a sort of puma came to growl at something outside.

The next morning he went with Estefan and Nando to cut some wood to build a house for Matilde and Javier, who were going to live together. They were married in the comarca, and that was recognized outside. He was dead tired, but also felt better than he had in a long time. The crew went to his house for a shower (the Indios are almost obsessively clean people) while he cooked a big pot of chicken with rice and a variety of vegetables. It reminded him he wanted to plant otoe and yampi – and chayote. There was culantro growing all over the place. He didn't use it much, because it could overwhelm other spices very quickly. There was a lot of albaca [Basil] and oregano.

Tomorrow, he would look over the layout for the water and sewer system. He had plenty 6" PVC tube for the main line of sewage. The water would be in 3/4" delivery, with ½" into the individual house. There was enough natural slant to the surface that the sewage would flow very well without pumping.

He slept exceptionally well. Estefan slept with him. It got very cool at night at that altitude.

He again thought of what gringos would think, and grinned. He knew the Indios thought nothing of it if anything happened. Nothing happened.

He wasn't sure how he would react. He meant to fit in, here. He just didn't think he would react, physically. He wasn't repulsed by the idea like in the states.

In the morning, Celia came to call that there was big trouble. Someone had opened the pen during the night and had killed a hog. She had no idea who would do such a thing! She had no idea of why they would do it.

Estefan was thoughtful. "Celia, did those ladrones from Panama try to get you to sell them your place?"

"Yes. I told them it was my place and would stay my place. This is not the comarca. I have a ROP, and I will not leave."

"Wait a minute! Someone is trying to buy land here?" Al asked. "There's plenty available, cheap, just a few hundred meters farther along! Why do they want your land?"

"I don't know. Maybe the silver? The government will take it if we dig up more than a little."

"There's silver here?"

"A little. There's a lot on the other side, but the government already took most of it," Estefan replied.

"If they try anything like this, I'll wrap their tails around a fence post! I was a cop in Georgia, and I can do a little investigation. I know some of the law from buying this place."

"Careful!" Estefan warned. "They're mafia! The police here are afraid of them!"

"Well, this cop isn't afraid of them! I won't put up with their shit for a millisecond!"

"Al, you are a friend. Please be very careful. It is not worth getting killed!" Celia cried.

Al nodded, then said he was going into David.

He asked them for any information they had about the people trying to steal their land.

"You can put most of the meat from the hog in the refri," Al said. "I'm damned glad I got the big side-by-side!"

<u>*David*</u>

Al got off the bus, then took a taxi to the police compound. He met Slvio Cantera, the head of violent crimes, and explained that there was no great amount of violence – yet, but they could expect it.

"Yes. We are very constrained about acting against the people trying to get in there," Silvio said, sadly. "It was not too long ago a friend who lives on the comarca helped with a problem when a number of the Ngobe Indios killed many judges and corrupt politicians. Several of the so-called mafia here became involved. They mostly killed each other.

"The top of the mountain is populated by Indios. I would think they would learn by now that one does *not* involve the Indios in such sordid issues.

"Do you know which individuals are doing these things?"

"All I know is that they are trying to get a section of land that may or may not have a lode of silver on it, and have started the crap. The people who have ROP certified there say they will not leave their land.

"You know how that turned out in the past, particularly under Noriega.

"Don Ronaldo Veras and Velma Quinteros were mentioned, and some bienes raizes company."

"Hmmm. Naldo V. and Diabla Q. I know of them. Very bad news, and from Colombia, not Panama.

"I could act against them for that, alone – except a judge has already declared them special friends of Panama who are above the law that says foreigners may not deal in bienes raizes.

"The only thing I can say is that, should the natives take the matter into their own hands, a judge has already ruled that I may not interfere, if you understand?"

"Let their corruption work against them. Okay. Just so we're clear."

"Al, these are mafia. It is not nearly what the term means in the states, but they are very dangerous people. Be most careful!"

"I've had to deal with the mafia in the states. As you say, these are amateurs. I know a few tricks."

"I see you have permisos for ... two pistols and two rifles, and a shotgun. In getting the permisos, slugs were taken for ID of the weapons, and the firing pin indent of the twelve guage?

"Please be certain that, should those weapons be used by someone else who, perhaps, stole them from you, it will lead directly to you, should you have not previously filed with the police that the items were stolen."

"I'll be damned sure nothing that would match my guns turns up in any violent or criminal action. I was with the police for some years, and know how such things are used in identification.

"Would you like a cup of drinkable coffee? This slop is purely disgusting!"

Silvio stood, picked up his hat, told the intercom he would be out of the office for an hour or so on a confidential police matter, and waved at the door.

They became solid friends while having coffee and dulces at a nearby fonda. Al learned a lot about how things were done here – and which cops to not trust under any circumstances.

None of those cops were in Silvio's department. They were mostly on rotation from Panama City, where the real base of corruption was.

Al bought a few things in the police supply store. He had the certification that would allow that since he came to Panama.

He then went back to Chorcha. This time, he took an ATV to the top. He had the money, and this was on sale at Ho Fai, it would serve well on the almost-road to the top. And it was a *lot* faster than a four hour hike, particularly while carrying about eighty pounds of ... stuff.

Jorge and Santos, another boy about 10 years old, met him and asked what all those little cameras and the funny cone-shaped things were for.

"To make it hard for cockroaches and other vermin to come on the property."

"One vermin is already here," Santos said, drily. "La Diabla and some snake they call Spike."

"They are talking to Paula about her land. She says they can buy it. For ten million balboas. Cash. No checks, that always bounce with them. Non-negotiable," Jorge said, with a grin.

"Sounds reasonable to me!" Al said, and tousled his hair.

There was the sound of a shot. Al grabbed a pistol from the cabinet drawer and bolted toward the sound. It was half a kilometer away, but he got there relatively quickly, to find Paula being held by a big black thug, and a woman in a dress suit snarling into her face. There was a dog laying dead on the path to the house.

Al didn't hesitate. He ran directly to the thug, who was trying to pull a pistol from his pocket, which meant he had to release Paula. He hit the thug hard enough to have broken his neck if he hadn't been moving away.

Paula wasn't a small woman. She went for the woman who was yelling into her face and decked her. Indio women almost never fight, but they do not go for the "pull hair and slap" bit. She threw a punch, shoulder behind it, that would have made a boxing coach proud. The woman went down like a sack of sand.

The thug had lunged at his pistol that he'd dropped when he was hit. Al came down on the hand holding the gun with his heavy boot. It mangled the hand, then the boot to the face, and both of them were unconscious and bleeding.

Paula picked up a Styrofoam cup of chicha from the rail and threw it into the woman's face. The woman sat up and screeched as Paula grabbed her hair and said, "You said you would mess up my face so people would scream if they saw me coming? You mean like this?" She pounded her three times in the face, breaking her nose and possibly a cheekbone. She dropped the woman and told Santos to bring two horses. They slung the two unconscious people on the horses, then Santos was told to take them to the gate by the entrance road and dump them off. Leave them and bring back the horses.

Al said to wait a minute. He got a piece of paper from Paula, and a marker pen. He wrote, *You want a war? You got it! – IA*

"Drop this on them before you come back." Santos grinned. Jorge said he would go with Santos. They would drop the ladrones beside the pickup truck they came in. He would put the note in the truck.

The horses and kids were heading away. Paula asked, "Who is IA? It's not you."

"The amateur mafia here are as scared of the Russian mafia as the real mafia in the states are. The Russians are crazy. Ivan Armakov, in Panama City, is supposed to be the head of the Russian mob. Actually, I meant Isaac Asimov. Too bad if they choose the wrong one, huh?"

She laughed. "So! Who is Isaac Asimov?"

"A scientist and writer in the states.

"Got anymore chicha? I'm thirsty. I wish you hadn't spilled it."

She laughed again and gave him the finger. She said she had some more. "And Al, I know this is serious, and very dangerous for us. I am very glad you are here. We would not know how to resist them."

They went to the house and had some chicha and

chatted about a lot of things. It seemed the silver was a fairly large vein. These ladrones didn't know exactly where it was, only that it was close to this place. It was on three people's land. No one would care if they took it, so long as they didn't leave an open sore in the Earth and left a little for when there was an emergency.

Al said he would like to see it. Maybe there was a way or three that everyone could come out ahead.

Al went back to his place. The whole Indio village would be on the watch for anyone not known who came to the mountain.

He spent what little was left of the day setting up the detectors and cameras and hooking them all to his TV recorder system. He didn't lie to himself as to whether this was over.

It wasn't.

It was after four in the morning when Al's phone rang. He looked at the ID and grinned. "Privado." This would be from the so-called mafia, and would be a threat.

"Habla."

"Mr. Al Vernon? New resident on Chorcha Mountain?"

"Yes. Who are you?"

"I am Vasily Armakov, in Panama City. Is it true you threatened that bunch of amateur wannabes with my brother's name?"

"I threatened someone? With your brother's name? I don't think so. I would surely remember that. I don't threaten anyone unless it's with my own name.

"I'm very surprised it's you calling. I expected ... someone else, entirely."

"I don't mind. I am sick and tired of those idiots keeping on trying to move in on me, particularly after I've gotten out of most of the bullshit big bad gangster routine.

"Actually, it does me a favor. That crud just

called and whined that they aren't trying to do anything that would blah, blither, blat. Shows they know I can swat them and still get a bit of sleep before dawn.

"Want to tell me what it's about?"

"They're using the old strongarm threats to steal some Indios' land."

"Really? Why?"

"There's some silver somewhere on it, or something."

"There is? I hadn't heard. Over near David? There's always a little coming in from the comarca ... Chorcha. Right against the comarca. They make rings and like that with silver. Somebody trying a salted mine bit on somebody else?"

"You sound reasonable. I'm surprised. There's a lode. Medium-sized, I think, though I haven't seen it. I want to be left alone, and for my friends to be left alone. If they want to mine the silver for their use, it's okay. For some hotshot piece of shit to take it – ah-ah!"

"Hmmm. You sound like a dear friend from that area. Even I wouldn't want to cross him. He's honest, and you just can't fight that, in the long run.

"Tell you what! How about I come look at the place. We might make a deal, like the one over by

Puerto Armuelles. I get the crap and pay them a set amount, and guarantee to restore any property damaged.

"See, I learned that you come out way better with that kind of business deal. I even get a special rate from the government, and nobody's in some stupid war that don't prove nothing.

"I can be there ... let's see ... nothing on my calendar for today and tomorrow ... about noon.

"Can I land the chopper ... yeah.

"If that's okay? I'll goddamned well guarantee those shitheads won't ever bother you or your friends again. I can do that by mentioning a name they'd rather face me than him, and they whine and cry because they're scared shitless they might make *me* mad."

"Well ... might be fun! I think you can land at the park at the entrance road. I can meet you in my ATV. Won't be any Rolls Royce to carry you around up here."

Vasily laughed. "I think I'll like you. See you around noon." He rang off.

Well! *That* was a surprise! Al was more surprised because he thought he would like the head honcho of the Russian mob!

He was just back asleep when a warning buzzer sounded, so he checked the surveillance monitor.

A figure was just slipping behind the bodega. It had a rifle.

Al sighed. He didn't expect that until tomorrow night. These people didn't ever do what he thought!

Oh, well. He got up and put on some dark clothes, using only the moonlight. He took the Glock 40, checked it, and went quietly out the front door, around the thick novio hedge, and was soon four feet away from the back of the bodega by the cut the walk went through.

A large figure stepped out the door of the bodega, holding the rifle, looked around carefully, then set the rifle in the branches of the guava tree, pointed toward the house. He then picked up an old pan and tapped it with a stick, just loud enough to be heard at the house.

Al silently stepped through the cut to see – a figure come up behind the rifleman and smack him over the head with a piece of rerod or pipe or something.

Like I said. These people never do what I expect! "Well! You got here two seconds before me!"

Obilio turned and grinned. "I didn't know you were here! You're pretty good!"

"Did you kill him?"

"I don't think so. I didn't hit him that hard. It

would mean the police would come here and we would spend three days trying to explain.

"What should we do with him?"

"Well, it'll be daylight in about an hour. There's enough moonlight.

"Maybe dump him at the gate, like the others?"

"With a note?"

"No. Just with all the bullets out of the gun. I'll check to see what backups he's carrying."

Al quickly checked him over, took his cedula, gave Obilio the two hundred dollars in the wallet. Kept the .25 automatic pistol and the sheath knife, and said he was ready to transport.

"Why did you give me the money?"

"Call it payment for security services."

"Okay."

Al didn't know why, but he hugged Obilio and helped sling the man over the horse when it came.

"Oh! I meant to tell you! There's a big Russian mafia boss coming to see me today. He'll land a helicopter near the gate. I'll meet him with the ATV."

"He's coming here? Why?"

"I'm making a deal for the silver. I don't see why I can't get rich, seeing somebody's going to."

Obilio laughed and gave him the finger, then walked away with the horse and passenger.

Al shook his head. He loved these people. He really loved these people.

"Twenty feet smaller and we couldn't land here," Vasily greeted. "What a view!

"You Vernon? I'm Vasily. The pilot's Eduardo."

"Al. This is Obilio. He's the one who gave the crud over there the love tap. I thought his buddies would have taken him away before this – or that he'd regain consciousness."

"Ed! Check the crud over and see if he's dead! You know who he is?"

"Cedula says Carlos Ramirez. I'd say a fractured skull. He's alive. Maybe a depressed concussion. Got a glass of water to see if he's better off dead?"

Vasily said there was water in the bottles in the chopper. Ed got a bottle and dumped it over the thug's head. He opened his eyes, which didn't want to focus.

"Concussion," Ed said. He shook his fingers close to the guy, who slowly focused.

"Who sent you?" Ed asked. The guy just looked confused. He passed out.

"Want I should take him to David while you fuck around up here?" Ed asked.

"Okay. Tell them he fell on a rock or something.

Be back by about four."

"Okay." Ed picked the guy up, with Obilio's help, and dumped him in the chopper. Ed asked Obilio if he'd like to go along to explain that he flagged down the chopper because he found the unconscious thug by the path.

Obilio said he'd never been in an airplane, much less a helicopter. It would be fun.

Al and Vasily got on the ATV and headed for Al's place. They would have a bit of a meal, then they would have Paula show them the lode.

Al had some chicken slow cooking in a sort of combination smoker/rotisserie thing he'd made. He had broccoli-cauliflower-celery, wok-fried in garlic oil, and mashed potatoes. Vasily said he hadn't had a meal that good in months, and he ate only in the best restaurants.

They got to know each other. Neither was quite what the other expected.

They walked to Paula's, and she took them about a kilometer into the mesa to a small cave, where they found there was a vein of silver that was a bit larger than Al expected – but nothing was quite like he expected here from the get-go.

"This was right here, all the time? Anyone can come and get what they want?" Vasily asked, confused.

"No," Paula replied. "Anyone we don't want here never comes here."

"I mean, there isn't any reason to make a big, ugly, poisoned hole here! We could take it in a wheelbarrow to the gate and fly it out in the chopper!

"Silver is about $530 a kilogram, now. It won't cost anything to dig it. How about I split up the middle? You dig it, I sell it?"

"A kilogram?" Paula asked. "There are a lot of kilograms here. What would we do with that much money? I am not council. You will have to deal with them. Part is on my land, and I know the law here is not like the comarca, and I can say it is mine, but I am Ngobe, and will say it is the property of the people here. The Ngobe and Al."

"We can save it for when there's an emergency and to build a school and clinic or whatever for the people here," Al suggested. "One tenth of it will stay for when the individual person wants to buy something, like now."

"I think the council will agree. They did with two places in the comarca before. Clint made the agreements."

"Ah! Clint would do that!" Vasily said.

"Who is this 'Clint' person?" Al asked. "I keep hearing about him. Those mystery books aren't real, actually ... are they?"

"He is a dear friend, a Ngobe," Vasily said. "He works with the law and anyone who will be fair. He is a real and true person who cares more for others than himself."

They spent about an hour trying to determine how much ore was there. No one was an expert, and no "expert" would come there. The lowest estimate was $500,000.

And Paula said there were several other, smaller lodes, but they weren't so easy to reach. She would like for them to take it all away so there wouldn't be anyone trying to steal their land.

Al took Vasily back to the chopper at about five o'clock. Obilio said he really liked the chopper. Ed had let him pilot a little, and it was great fun. Ed said Obilio was a natural pilot.

When they were getting on the chopper to go, Obilio and Ed held each other for a long time, it seemed. Ed said he would come to visit when he had the time. Al raised an eyebrow at Vasily, who laughed. "I didn't know. It's none of my business. I hope they had as good an afternoon as I did!"

Al and Obilio went back to Al's place, where Jorge and Santos were waiting to see what had happened.

"We all had a great time, and I think there will

be an agreement that serves all well," Obilio said. "I flew a chopper! Ed is a very special person, and a very good teacher!"

Al had to grin at that.

Things went along very smoothly for the next few days. Vasily made an agreement with the people on the mesa, and they were carrying about fifty kilos of silver to the landing place every day. They had it in a little cement block container they could lock. When they had 200 kilos, Al called Vasily, who sent the chopper for it. Ed wasn't piloting, and Al asked why.

"Ed? He's Vasily and Ivan's private pilot."

Four days later the chopper came early, and Vasily was on it. He said he liked the area. It was magnificent for the view, cooler than lower altitudes, and the people treated him like the guy next door instead of some monster they wanted to hide from. He got a giggling fit when he ordered that Estaban bring him something that he could get by walking twenty feet. Esteban said, "Fuck you!" and gave him the bird.

"I think I love these people as much as you do! I'm so used to people falling all over themselves to do me a favor! These people are honest, and just say 'Fuck you!' and take it as a joke!"

He also got a kick out of Ed and Basilio going to Basilio's house for some chicha and fun. "In Panama, they would try to make it that I wouldn't guess. Here, they say we're going for some chicha and a roll in the hay!

"Didn't Obilio say he has a wife who had a baby?"

"Yes," Santos, who was there, but behind Vasily said. "She will get upset if they are together too much. I don't think that will happen. It's just fun, and they care about each other.

"Besides, Ed isn't here that much."

Vasily giggled at that. "I love these people! I really do!

"Al, do you have a boyfriend?"

"Me? No. I suppose I could. Here. Back in the states, I would get all huffed up if anyone suggested it."

"Ah, life among the innocents. I wish I could start over again. I envy the innocence of these people. They don't fight against life, they live it!

"Would that I could."

"I did the best thing I ever did when I moved here."

"Al, could you find me a little place here where I could come to disappear and hide away? I would just want a little place like Paula's. Nothing fancy, and no one would believe I could be there."

"Why not Paula's?" Jorge asked. "She really likes you. She says you're fun."

"You mean ... marry her?"

"No. That's silly. If you get along and want to get married, that's later. She divorced Jaime when he wanted to live in Panama City. Her son and daughter are living on the comarca. They're like her. They don't like cities.

"If you're married, she would say no."

"My wife died of cancer six years ago, and my kids are grown and on their own.

"Could you believe I'm actually considering it!?

"Al, are you in that kind of deal with Yveth?"

"We stay together some. I think I'll marry her, if she wants to."

"Well! Maybe I would like to talk with Paula awhile. She's a solid woman, and I like solid women, because she will be like Esteban and say, 'Fuck you!' when I'm being an ass."

They chatted a few minutes, then Vasily went to Paula's and Al and Santos went to his place to figure where the best place would be to plant the guanabana and marmonchina. As it was starting to get dark, Vasily and Ed went to the chopper to head back to Panama City.

Vasily would come back the next trip and stay

with Paula for as long as he could get away with it. Al said to be careful, because that much time with Obilio would start to grind on his wife.

"I know," Ed said. "We're just very close friends. I won't cause trouble."

"There are a lot of handsome guys here – if you want company," Vasily said, and giggled.

"Oh, I'll stay with Al!" Ed shot back.

"Yveth might have something to say about that," Al said.

"Who cares what she might say?"

"Me."

"Actually, Ed will fly the silver back and come for me when I call, so even that's not a problem," Vasily said. "I told Ivan all about this place. He doesn't understand how I wouldn't go crazier than I already am, living away from the city.

"He says to take pictures. He doesn't want to actually come here."

They joked a bit, then left.

It was three months later when they took the last of the silver they were going to take from the lode. Vasily had found two more smaller lodes, but decided they could stay there. He had fifty times the money he could spend if he just dropped it off the chopper. He stayed with Paula for a week at the time. Things were very peaceful and easy. Al liked the way of the people. He had just helped Esteban and Santo load an old pickup with three varieties of avocados to take into David to the vegetable market. It was mangos last week, and yuca the week before. They brought back enough rice and flour and such to take care of everyone.

The people shared. They had no use for money, and had more than $600,000 in the bank and about $20,000 Berto kept to give them what they needed when they wanted to buy anything. The water delivery system was in and working, as was the sewer system. Al had placed some solar panels, and everyone who wanted electricity could have it, though most didn't want it.

Just two days ago Yveth moved back to the comarca. Al truly wished her the best happiness. She was a special woman, but she wanted a family, and Al didn't.

Al talked with Vasily about the problems that could arise because of the ROP status of the people. Vasily had Ivan check on a way to insure there wouldn't be any problems in the future [as much as that was possible here]. They could have the land titled for $32.00 per hectares, in large lots.

The people didn't want titles. That meant they owned the land, and owning things was no part of their culture.

"Vasily, this is an impossible situation. The culture clash. It could...." Al started. "Vasily! Ask Ivan if the title could be bought by a corporation for the same price!"

Vasily asked. "Yes. What's the plan?"

"We form a corporation! A holding corporation! Every person on this part of the mountain is an equal partner. The corporation holds title, and they can't be dispossessed!"

Vasily talked with Ivan for a few minutes. "Al, Ivan will set up the corporation. It will cost sixteen hundred dollars, and the renewal fee will be six hundred dollars a year.

"I'll pay that! If I was to pay rent in Panama City for a room in a house like Paula's, it would be two hundred a month, so it's a lot cheaper than rent!

"I'll be the head of the corporation, of course!"

"Fuck you!" Paula said, bringing in chicha for everybody. "*I'll* be jefe, and you will do as I say or I'll vote you out!"

They teased and played for awhile, but Al knew it would be done. This would be about 980 hectares, the way the plots of ROP added up.

A week later, while Ivan was working with the lawyers, some people from farther along the mesa came in to ask Al what they should do. They heard he had helped the people on "this end" of the mesa, and there were some people who were trying to make them sell their land to a company.

Al called Vasily, who came over to listen. He found the company on his computer, *Cielos Paraisos Privados,* a real estate company operating out of Colon.

Vasily darkened several shades, pure fury radiating from him. "Guess who these shithead bastards are?" he hissed.

"Velma Dearest and Company?" Al asked.

"You got it! I warned them!

"Al, we prepare for a war. Literally. Anyone from that company steps foot on this mountain, it is the last step they ever take, except the one into Hell!"

"Vas, call Ivan! Fast! I want to talk with him!"

Vasily punched the autodial for Ivan's private number. He said Al wanted to talk about the problem here.

"Ivan, can you make a deal for the whole top of this mountain? For agricultural use, only. I think there's a special rate for that. We can get twelve five or so with what we've got on hand at thirty two. I think the top of the mountain is about seventeen thousand. Can we get it all for six hundred grand?"

"I think so. I will add whatever is necessary. I'm sure Vasily will agree to that. It will only cost four hundred more for the corporation and a hundred more per renewal."

Vasily reached for the phone, put it on speaker, and said, "Ivan, expand it to the base of the mountain. Put ten million in the corporation as a loan without interest from us. Due date, one hundred years, renewable at their option."

"Done! I see you are not bored, living in the jungle with the savages!"

"Fuck you!" Esteban said.

"I heard when you put it on speaker. I find Vasily was correct when he told me it was a charge to have someone tell you to fuck off! No one here has the nerve!"

"Everyone here does! They say it all the time. I do too!

"Ivan, because of who they are, I'm ready for a war to the end."

"It will last two minutes.

"Did you know that La Diabla spent more than thirty thou for the plastic surgery to get her face fixed? Could that be behind it?"

"Part of it, I suppose. I don't think she knows the Indios up here keep in contact. There's about three kilometers of jungle between that end and this. There's a path, but they mostly meet in Los Angeles and David. She thinks no one will tell me they're there. She could have had someone tell her that my chopper comes here a lot. She's stupid enough to think she can get me alone up here and knock me over, and you won't know who was behind it."

"She's about that dumb. I'll have La Tigra keep a close eye on her. One word, she's history, and a very small footnote there."

"I hate getting back into this crap, but *no one* is going to threaten my friends!"

They talked a bit longer, then rang off.

"Well, this could be most interesting!" Vasily declared. "I haven't been in a position where I'm actually in any danger since I was twenty years old! It's sort of exciting, in a negative way."

"We have it sewed," Vasily reported. "The corporation is complete, and the entire mountain, except for the falls, of course, are private property. The only exceptions are the two ranch owners, and that is just forty one hectares at the entrance. We could have claimed that, but stated, officially, that we don't do business that way, but they will have to maintain the property according to the law. They haven't maintained it in any way for the past eight years, so it could be technically seized. The Arrends ass said he was going to put a toll booth where the road ends, so we filed an eviction notice. He signed a six meter wide piece for a public access road. He backed off, but we can expect future trouble.

"He's just the type our enemy will try to use.

"Veras and Quinteros are laying low. They don't know I'm involved, but they suspect it, seeing I'm on the corporation. I think they were just going to get revenge on Al and Paula, then found out I stay here. They may guess about the silver, but that is something they can't check.

"There is a man called Enrique Domingo, from Argentina, involved with them, and a man called Marty Leven, from the states. Leven is on his way to David right now. Aeroperlas.

"Al, they've found something else up here. They would not be doing this, taking the chances, for a lousy half mil."

"I've been wondering about that. I don't know what it is. There's usually a lode of another heavy metal where there's silver, but I don't know what it could be that the people wouldn't know about. If my information is correct, there is uranium near a silver mine in the Puerto Armuelles area. I don't think it's that. There will be lead, but not much. Maybe some copper.

"I have no idea what it could be."

"There was a geological survey about five or six years ago. They didn't note anything. I'll have a couple of guys with a Geiger counter look around the place. Maybe a sensitive metal detector."

"We'll wait for that. I want to concentrate on the ones doing it more than what it is."

"We're watching every move. They don't know it.

"Do you have a way for the people to contact you if anyone comes?"

"Yes. It's something they know about, but don't

know about, if you get the drift."

Vasily thought a minute, then smirked. "The phones almost every one of them carry?"

Al nodded. "And a couple of those walkie-talkies the linemen carry. And code phrases that sound like chat."

"Then we wait."

"Yo! Vas! Paula!" Al called as he went to Paula's house two mornings later. Vas came out in the porch and said, "Contact?"

"Yep! Four people no one knows are hiking up the road from Los Angeles. Look like backpackers, but are too well shaped, physically, for those types. At least two of them are armed. From Sylvia Flores, in Los Angeles. Her brother is security guard at the milk farm where the path starts. They went by at five twenty, before anybody except the milking machine men were there to bring in the cows."

"Hmm. Three and a half hours, if they're that fit. I wonder if there's some kind of plan to distract you and me, hmm?"

"Well, it's six ten, so they'll have to try it before eight. That means before seven thirty. I'll be waiting for anything."

Al went back toward his house. He was almost

there when his phone, the one a lot of people knew the number for, buzzed.

"Habla."

"Mr. Vernon? I'm Marty Leven. I took a chance calling this early, but would like to request that you come to David to meet with me this morning.

"I know it seems an imposition, but it has to do with your pension."

Al grinned. He didn't care about the pension anymore [but he wouldn't refuse it]. Leven was from the states, and Al was an ex-cop, so the mobs would know a lot about him.

"I have some things to do, but could maybe come about eleven or so?"

"If you can make it earlier? I'm sorry, but I have to contact several people later, in Santiago. It takes four hours to get there, and I'm to meet them at three thirty, so you can see why I'm in a hurry. It's really a simple matter of your signature with a notary."

"Okay. If I leave here at seven thirty I can be there by ten or so. Call you at this number ... oh. It's privado, so I can't do that."

"I'm so sorry! I forgot! I'll call you back immediately so you will have the number!"

He rang off, there was a short pause, then the phone buzzed again with a number in the ID window. Al said he had it, and would mark it. He'd call when he reached the terminal in David.

He called Vasily on his other phone and told him about the call and gave him the number.

"I wonder if they'll contact me – or if I'm the one to be eliminated?"

Al laughed. "They don't know these people, and badly underestimate them. As La Diabla did!"

"You going to David?"

"Might as well. Maybe I'll actually meet this Leven joker. Maybe I'll even sign a phony paper for the notary!"

"I'll have Ed take you to the airport! You can surprise them by turning up early – in my chopper!"

They both got a laugh at that.

Al cleaned up and changed, had a couple of cups of rich strong coffee, and went out to join Ed to ride the ATV to the chopper. They were landing in Malek at 9:15. Al called and said he'd just got there, that a friend was on the way to Panama City and had dropped him off.

Leven sounded sacred, even on the phone. "Er, that's good news. It gives a little more time.

"Uh, friend? Gringo?"

"No. Panamanian. I think he and his brother are from Latvia or somewhere, originally. They have some businesses and helped us with a sort of, what you might call, legal problem.

"I'll grab a taxi. Where can I meet you?"

"Er, that is ... I'm at the Ciudad de David. In the restaurant? I need some coffee and eggs or something."

"Okay! About half an hour. I could use some breakfast, myself."

He flagged a cab. Ed was laughing. The radio came on in the chopper. It was Vasily, saying he had a hack to the number Al gave him. That number was very busy, at the moment, first to Colon, then to a dead signal area near Chiriqui.

On the cab, Vasily called him. "What did you tell him? They're in a panic because they think I'm going to Panama City."

"Then they are on their way up there to knock you over."

"I don't ... they're terrified because I'm on my ... Al! I'll call in a few minutes! They planned to knock over Ivan and me, both! That has to be it! There's no way any of them could survive ten minutes if they just get one of us!

"Al! Leven is probably going to try to knock you over – or *was*! Now he'll meet you in a public place to show it was just a business meeting and coincidence, hah, hah!"

"The best laid plans of fools and idiots can sometimes go awry! I think I'll really enjoy making this Leven character squirm!

"Vas, he *has* to go to Santiago now! This is rich!"

"Hah! He's using his phone right now to book a seat on the Santiago bus!

"This has gotten to be fun!"

"Vas, there's no way to call that bunch going up there. It's a dead signal area for a lot of that side of the mountain. Be damned careful!"

"Covered. Later."

Al rang off. The cab dropped him at the entrance to the hotel. He went to the restaurant and looked around. A man who looked just a bit too much like a thug saw him and waved. He went to the table.

He had pictured Leven as a more timid, smaller type. Suave and amiable. This one looked like a lifeguard at a rundown beach in a suit that didn't fit quite right.

"I'm in a confused mess!" Leven cried. "They made the appointments too close together, and didn't even contact you!"

"Yeah. Bureaucrats sitting in an office in Detroit, looking at a map, and saying it was close. They didn't know about the trail down the mountain. Raised in rate to the level of their incompetency.

"What's this about my pension? I thought all that was handled."

"Er, oh. that. As you say, the level of their incompetency. Everything handled, page and paragraph! Have a nice day! Maybe we'll meet again!

"Then they note, after you were gone from the state, Hell! from the country! They forgot to have you sign the release form, so they've been paying you illegally, and their ass is in a crack!

"So they spend a few thou sending me to get a signature! I said they should just forge it. You damned well weren't going to object!

"I'm sorry I ever got involved. If I leave, I lose *my* pension!"

They chatted a minute. Al said they didn't have much time, and that they might be caught at the notary for awhile in line, as he'd learned when he bought his place.

"Well, it's not like, I mean, we can get two witness signatures, yours and mine, and they can file it. That's what they do in the main office, as you know from going through the shit."

Leven called over the waiter and asked that he get one other to witness a contract. He put a paper on the table that looked like what it was – a 5 cent copy machine form. Al thought of telling him he signed originals, not copies, but decided it wasn't worth the effort:

This is to certify that I, <u>Alton Martin Vernon</u> give release for funds to be disbursed according to the affixed contract with the Policemen's Pension Fund held in The Bank of America. date: . / / .

Signed: Witness 1   Witness 2

He almost laughed out loud. He scribbled a signature that didn't look at all like his, the two waiters signed it, Leven gave each of them a dollar, and put the form in a little briefcase.

"Well! All that, and I fly from San Die ... California here for eight hundred bucks, stay in a eighty dollar a night hotel, go to Santiago to go through it again, then go home. Efficiency!

"I guess I'd better get my bag and head for the bus. It's been hectic, but not bad."

"I have to go to the terminal, too. I'll walk with you. David really is a nice town, but it's turning into a city, and they're all alike"

"Er, that will be, yes. Five minutes!" Leven went to the elevator. Al waited and called Vasily, who said the four were about ten minutes from the top. He'd wait and see what they did before doing anything himself. He might just let it be, if they didn't try anything with Ivan. He would damned well have a message or two to deliver. It would be about fifteen minutes for them to come through the jungle to Paula's house. They might get a signal at the top and a call, and just go back.

Leven came back with a suitcase, turned in his key, paid the bill with a credit card, and he and Al walked to the Santiago-David terminal. Leven got on the bus, and Al waited until it pulled out to head for the terminal himself.

He was almost to Chiriqui when Vasily called.

"Al, they went directly to the path. Nando was watching. They got a call and argued, then came on down the path. One of them saw Nando, so he went on and passed them when they sat on the rocks. He acted like he was arguing with his girlfriend on the phone, and said 'Bueno!' when he passed them. He's coming on, because it would look suspicious if he turned back now. They started coming on. They're about six or eight minutes away. We've got all your guns, and are waiting. I had Ed fly on toward Panama City. He can come for me when I call."

"I'll be there in about ... have Santo bring the ATV down. I don't want to spend four hours hiking up there today."

"I'll call when they get to the village."

Al caught the Tole bus and had to sit next to a fat woman with a baby. She grinned and giggled and batted her eyes at him. He ignored her.

He was just past Chiriqui when his phone buzzed: "Al, two of them stopped a few meters back, and two are coming up the path. Tomas is there. They asked him something. He said something. The big one is ... MATAR EL MATAR EL! [there were the sounds of shots] Al! They hit ... I hope he's not hurt bad. It was a judo chop or karate or something. He's just a fifteem year old kid! I'll kill the bastards with my own hands!" Al could hear him yelling to not let the other two get away. There were more shots, a pause, and more.

"I'm hit, but not serious, I think. Al, they shot little Jorge! Oh, dear god I don't believe in, let him be alright.

"Get up here! I want Leven hit the second he gets off that bus, Santiago or anywhere else!

"I'm getting a call from Ivan. Later."

Al hit the road on the run when the bus stopped. Santos was just getting there. He jumped on the ATV and said to get them to the top yesterday! Santos said he head some shots, he thought.

It took twenty four minutes to reach the top, then

four to get to Paula's place. Tomas had a sort of neck brace on. "Just sprained," Luisa said.

"Jorge?"

"Serious. They have taken him to Los Angeles. I think ... I don't know. It is very serious."

"Vasily?"

"Tonta! He's shot, and is helping take the dead malditos to throw in the falls! Tonta! The men can do that!"

He hugged Tomas for a long moment and went outside to see Vasily and Julio coming up from the path to the falls. Vasily was staggering a bit.

"Lost some blood. Lay down and try to relax. Talk later. Ivan is okay. Four there, too."

Paula put him on the bed and made a bandage. "It's stopped bleeding. All the way through, so I think he'll be alright. Bring me some of the altimise and some guayaba extract. I have the bread mold."

Al raced to his house and got the medicines he kept for when needed.

Paula said he would be alright, but would probably limp a little. It went through the upper leg.

Tomas came to lay against him. He said, "Uncle Vas, we love you." Vasily hugged him and passed out.

Al cried.

"Well! I can do with a little less excitement in my life!" Vasily said, two days later. "I'm still weak, but my body needs to make a lot of blood. No transfusion up here!

"Tomas is much better. Jorge will be alright, but will have a scar to brag about. I don't think I'll brag about my own. I should know better.

"Paula said you cried for us. It takes a very strong man to care enough about others to cry when you're afraid they're hurt.

"Al, I love these people more every day. I used to be the world's worst asshole, because I didn't understand them. They are every one better persons than I am. I hope to change that!

"Now! We both know who brought this on. They are in hiding in Colon, because they can use the violent culture there against other people. Four Colon thugs here, four in Panama City, for Ivan. Only Leven wasn't from Colon.

"It seems he got off the bus in Santiago and went to the banos. He must have fallen and hit something, because he had a broken neck. Such lovely people should be more careful.

"What can we do about those three people?"

"We'll have to figure some way to get them to

come here, or I'll have to go to Colon.

"Vas, there's something up here they want. They didn't go through all that just to get rid of you and Ivan. It doesn't make sense!"

"I almost forgot about that. I'll have the guys in my organization trace every move and every word from her since a year before she came up here."

"I think since a week before she came up here. She was after silver, and found something else. I wonder ... did she ever go to the mine?"

Vas called Paula. Yes. She went there once, and said it was worth going after. When Al came was her second time she knew about, but there could have been a time before she didn't know about, because she *did* go to the mine.

"Vas, Hon, talk to the children. They would know."

Vas looked at Al, and said, "The kids know everything. Let's talk with a few of them.

"She knew about the trail from Los Angeles. It could be something between here and the village. It will be closer to here."

"It will be here," Al replied. "She was trying to get the land here."

They went into the council area, where several children were drying the cacao and coffee. Vas asked them about the evil woman who came before.

"She came with that big black man twice. They were on the path to Oeste Puebla," a girl about 6 years old said. "They tried to act like they were nice people who came to see the view. She acted like the Queen of Everywhere, so we knew they were mentirosas."

"What did they want?" Al asked. "I mean, really."

"Well, the black man wanted to know where the coins were," a small boy said. "They had one of those gold coins from a long time ago in another place."

"Gold coins? Ancient? Another place?" Vasily asked.

The kids shrugged. "There was a couple. From the altita. Benicio took one to David to buy some cloth."

Al nodded. "So. It figures, in a way. They think there's some kind of treasure up here.

"I doubt they'd come here ... with a coin that might be the only one dropped up here.

"Vas, let's get to the comps. I want to know some history of this place."

Vasily agreed. They thanked the children and headed back.

"What is this altita?" Vas asked.

"A little hill that sticks out a little bit higher than the surrounding land."

The computers didn't have much. A couple of conquistadores parties had climbed the mountain because it would be the perfectly defendable position. They didn't stay, because it was also very hard to climb and there was no water for three months of the year. Papers were cited. They were in Panama City, in the national museum.

Al downloaded PDFs of the four papers. Three of them were scripts by a Christian Vega, who was a leader of the parties, and one by Vicente Flores, who was a sort of record keeper for the parties,

It was hard reading. The papers were faded and in a script that was a bit rough.

Vega told of the climb near the waterfall on the side facing more westward. There was a bit about how difficult it was to carry the chest, but there was nowhere to leave it that could be considered even moderately secure.

The second was mostly about the view and how, considering the mountain was so hard to climb, it would be more defensible than any place they'd investigated.

The third was about how they were desperate for water. They had been there for more than a month, and there had been no rain. The waterfall had dried. There were no ponds or lakes, and all the small quebradas were dried. They would return to the lower area, much wiser.

The paper by Flores was far easier to read. It made a few passing remarks referring to earlier papers. It was about the lack of understanding of how much of their treasure had disappeared, then how there was great suspicion of Geraldo Crespira, who had been discovered with five coins from the missing booty. He was intercepted as he was starting down the trail to the lowlands. His descent was far more rapid than he planned, arriving at the bottom in less than a minute. None of the missing treasure was found before the party abandoned the mountain.

Al handed it to Vasily, who read it, and shook his head. "Benificio found a couple. The treasure is on altita," Vas said. "We have to talk to him."

They went to the center to find that Benicio was probably at his finca, about a half kilometer toward the center of the mesa. They took the ATV to the finca. Benicio was working in the meadow with the yuca.

"The little piece of the altita fell last year when we had the temblor and the hard rain. Sort of a small derumbe. There were three coins and a little pretty ring I gave to Joana [his wife]."

Al said they'd go to the altita to see if there were more coins. "Did you try to find more coins?"

"No. Why would I? I don't have use for more. I was thinking maybe I could find another ring, but didn't have time to look. I was only there to get the calf that had wandered away."

"You can't know how I love these people!" Vasily cried. "Maybe a million dollars worth of gold laying around, but no time to look for it because the calf wandered away and had to be taken back!"

Al laughed. They hugged Benicio and went on toward the altita.

Al's phone buzzed. It was Santos, who said there were some people with the policia who were trying to find somebody near the hill. They didn't know what to tell them.

"Tell them it is private property, so you will have them wait at the council area until I come. The police are not to enter the property unless they have a warrant. No weapons are allowed on the mesa.

"I will be there in fifteen minutes, with my vice-president of the corporation that has title to the property."

There was a pause.

"Arrends is with them. He says the police can come anytime they want."

"Only on his finca – that he has failed to maintain as per the agreement."

There was another pause.

"Arrends wants to come with the other people, and he says the policia are his guards. He is paying them, not the government, and he will bring them with him."

"Put the asshole on." Vasily demanded.

"Arrends here. I'll bring whoever I want, whenever I want!"

"Vasily Armakov here. You'll kiss my ass, and I'll still say you bring no weapons or policia, private or otherwise, onto the mesa. You will also maintain that property as agreed, or you will be evicted. You have ten days.

"Anything else, Ass-ends?"

"The road to the center is public property, as you declared. I'll bring whoever I want on it!"

"The part through your finca is the only part declared public. The public doesn't maintain the road, so it is corporate property. We are almost to the center, you are arguing where you came onto the mountain.

"Oh! One more item! It's now five days! Any part of the property not in the condition you agree on will become corporate property as of that date at this time. Got it?"

"You can't do this!"

"Yes, I can. We are five minutes from the center. If you do not arrive in a timely matter, we will assume you have decided the matter, whatever it is, wasn't worth the time."

There was the sound of a minor argument, then, "Mr. Comacho and three business associates – and me! – will be there in a few minutes."

"Give Santos his phone."

"Santos here, Vas. Arrends is telling the police to wait. He is telling them something else, too."

"Put your phone in your pocket. Don't turn it off," Al said.

"Yes. We will be there soon."

They waited. Most sounds from the phone were indistinct, except for a word here and there.

Vasily used his own phone to call Ivan and tell him what was happening, and that there was an old treasure chest somewhere on the land.

"Vasily, you *do* tend to get yourself into some ridiculous situations, don't you?" Ivan replied. "I think I envy you. I'm sitting here in this palace, ordering others, and perfectly safe, while you are running around playing protector of a bunch of Indios, and have even been shot once!

"Do you have any idea how useless I feel?"

They pulled into the center. Al had six of the local people in position, and armed. He said he didn't believe for a picosecond that these vermin weren't going to do something ultimately stupid.

Arrends came striding into the center with Santos behind and four other people in suits. Santos smirked at his back and grinned at Al.

"I don't have time to put up with this obstructionism!" Arrends snarled. "You are going to regret this! I promise. You don't know who I am!"

"You're a rather stupid asshole idiot who's in a mile over your head," Vasily said, reasonably. "What do you want?

"I am Vasily Armakov."

"Armakov is in Panama City. That is easy to check! You are a nobody!"

"I'm Mr. Vernon, to you. Ivan is in Panama City. Mr. Vasily Armakov is right here," Al said. "What do you want? What do you think you'll accomplish with this idiocy?"

The woman with the group called Arrends over. She said something in a panicky whisper, and Arrends turned to look at Vasily, sudden fear showing on his face.

"Well, Elisa, it seems your information is

lacking," Vasily said to her. "Al, this is Elisa Cartago, a person I have done business with in the past. She's a lawyer, so nothing else is needed, as to description.

"I suppose these other two clowns are lawyers, too. They look that insipid."

"Er, I'm Angel Velasco. I'm an attorney for Mr. Comacho, who is CEO of the Paraiso ..." He ran down.

"No! You mean ... I'm shocked! That crooked real estate company in Colon? Isn't that woman ... what was her name? ... Velma What-the-fuck-ever ... head of that bad joke?" Vasily asked, overdone shock radiating from him. [Al and Santos giggled] "What do you want, now?"

"Er, that is, we, um, the company for rights, uh to, you know."

"Shee! Even I couldn't translate *that* bit!" Al exclaimed.

"We wanted to make a legal agreement with a person who owns some property here," Velasco declared. "It's all perfectly legal!"

"So legal you have four phony cops along with you?" Santos asked. "Nobody owns any land here. That's stupid!"

"Uh, we were led to believe the people here were recently awarded title to the land they are residing upon, that was formerly ROP land," Cartago said, like she was reading a cue card.

"I'm glad she isn't *my* lawyer!" Santos cried. "I'd spend my whole life with my ass in a crack!" Al and Vasily laughed.

"All land on this mountain, except forty one hectares, is corporate-owned. Our stockholders and employees are granted free use," Vasily replied.

There was a cry like that of a brownwing falcon. Al said that was amazingly stupid, to think the guardia wouldn't be watched. "Are they actually policia off duty, or simply thugs you want to scare the people with? Do you really intend to attack Vasily Armakov?"

"I swear! We didn't think Armakov would be here! I swear!" Cartago cried.

"You just thought you could come here and terrorize the people with impunity," Al said acidly.

"Esteban! They are not policia. Either they turn back – now! – or they will not live to leave this mountain! If they bother any person here, they are to be shot!" Vasily called, loudly.

Arrends bolted. Santos tackled him. The others formed a tight wad, but didn't move.

There was the sound of automatic gunfire, then

some isolated shots, then automatic that was cut off abruptly.

"Esteban?!" Vasily yelled.

"Nilsa was shot. The soldiers are no more. I have a very small wound on my arm."

"How is Nilsa? Is she hurt bad?" Al yelled.

"She is dead."

Vasily took out his phone, pure fury on his face, punched a speed dial, waited a minute, then ordered, "Take the whole lot of them *out*, Ivan! *Now*! No recourse!" He rang off. "Al, should this bunch go over the falls without a barrel?"

Cartago screamed. Arrends was sobbing. The others were pleading.

"They go back to Panama City, Arrends included," Al suggested. "Word gets out to every enemy they have that they made a deal. The courts have been given a lot of evidence that will take some *very* big names off the roster with their guaranteed testimony. The Policia Nacional are at this moment forming squads to make arrests."

"Ah! Let them learn what it's like to be ... them!" Vasily agreed. He turned to them. "You can go. To Panama City. From there, you can go to any other country that will have you.

"The corporation files notice on the twenty eight hectares listed to Arrends for seizure. He failed to maintain it to the conditions in his exemption, thus loses that exemption.

"Anything else, Al? Santos?"

They shook their heads.

"This case is closed, but all persons involved will be carefully watched for a period of five hundred years or until they die – which will probably be closer to five days for most of them," Vasily declared. "We will meet here, the community, in one hour, to honor Nilsa, an honest and innocent woman, murdered by the worst kind of slime in the world."

They all nodded. The group of ladrones started walking, looking terrified and defeated, for the entrance road.

"Well, the treasure has been sent to Buabidi," Al said. "They have the pirate ship museum there, and this is, in all respects, a case of pirate treasure."

"The Velma group ceased to exist, in their entirety, within three hours of a phone call from someone out in the country somewhere. The representatives of the company, along with their accomplices, lived as much as nine days. They all had fatal and rather unpleasant accidents. Two major crime lords – not among them yours truly – got into an internal war and are now minor footnotes," Vasily continued. "Paula and I are married, as of this announcement, in the tradition of the Ngobe.

"If there is any more treasure or silver or anything else here that will bring that kind of disease to this mountain, find it, and we will make damned sure it is never a problem anymore."

"The most important thing that has happened is that we have new friends. With the things happening in the cities now, we are very lucky to be here. As we are in the most defendable place, save by air attack, in Panama," Bino said. "It is possible, noting what happened in the comarca with the big phosphate company, that even that can be defended very well.

"Al and Vas have said, many times, that they love the people.

"The people love them. They are part of us, of our community, and will always be."

"We are a community, not just people who live in the same place," Esteban said. "Okay! Enough silly speeches! Pass me a beer!"

"Paula! Hand me that beer there!" Vasily ordered.

"Fuck you!"

Everyone toasted to that with their beer.

C. D. Moulton's works are available on most major outlets as printed or e-books. CD writes the CD Grimes, PI, mysteries, the Det. Lt. Nick Storie mysteries, the Clint Faraday mysteries, the Flight of the Maita science fiction series, books on orchid culture and many others of many types. Mystery, adventure, intrigue, science fiction, humor, fantasy, paranormal, mild erotica, and factual.

www.ingramcontent.com/pod-product-compliance
Lightning Source LLC
Chambersburg PA
CBHW061335120726

48001CB00002B/882